Cash Kat

by Linda Joy Singleton

illustrated by Christina Wald

W9-BYM-291

WITHDRAWN

Kat kerplunks shiny pennies into her Kitty Bank as she waits on the porch.

Vroom! Gram Hatter's jeep roars up to the curb. "Ready for a treasure hunt, Kat?"

"Yes!" Kat jumps into the jeep.

Vroom! Roar! Off they go to clean up City Park.

"Keep a sharp eye out for buried treasure." Gram Hatter plucks a paper from her craft bag. She folds it into a hat.

A pirate hat for Kat.

"I'm Pirate Kat and I spy pirate loot." Kat picks up a penny.

Aye-aye matey! Find a penny, pick it up, all the day you'll have good luck.
Is one penny lucky enough to buy ice cream?

No.

You'll need more.

"This many?" Kat holds up five fingers.

Gram Hatter shakes her head. "Many, many more."

When Kat's trash bag is full, she spies something shiny. "A bigger penny!" she cries.

"A nickel," says Gram Hatter.

"One nickel equals five pennies," said Gram Hatter.

"Is that enough for ice cream?"

"Not yet." Gram Hatter folds a new hat.

Keep looking, Explorer Kat.

Explorer Kat stalks through wild flowers and finds a silver coin that's smaller than the penny and nickel. Gram Hatter says it's a dime.

"It's little." Kat frowns.

"It may be little but it's worth twice as much as a nickel," Gram Hatter explains.

It takes ten pennies or two nickels to equal one dime.

Kat holds up ten fingers and counts them like pennies.

Gram Hatter folds paper triangles into a crown hat.

You are rich like a queen. Here's your crown.

I am Queen Kat and I search my kingdom for coins.

Queen Kat picks up a soggy shoe from the stream and three silver coins roll out. "Royal jewels. These are even bigger than nickels and dimes," Kat says.

Quarters. It takes five nickels, or two dimes and one nickel, to equal a quarter.

WITHDRAWN

But it still isn't enough to buy ice cream.

So Gram Hatter helps look as they pick up trash. They crawl through weed jungles, lift monster rocks and search in a sand box.

They don't find any more coins, but Kat finds treasure—a dollar bill!

"Amazing! You need a special hat for your lucky day." Gram Hatter folds a paper hat that has two pointy ears and a long tail. "A cat hat for Kat."

 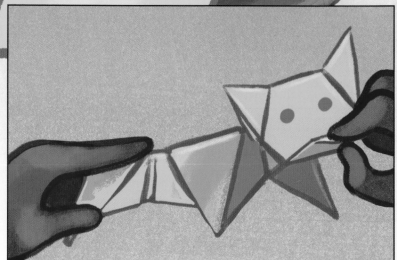

They turn in their bags of trash and a lady with a feather hat thanks them for their help.

Kat points to a glass jar on the table. "What's that for?"

"It's to collect money to help beautify the park," the woman answers.

Kat looks around. The park benches need new paint, the swing set is missing a swing, and the grass has brown patches.

Kat jingles the coins in her hand and smooths the dollar bill.

Kat kerplunks the shiny coins into the donation jar. Then she folds the dollar bill and slides it through the slot.

"Big hearts are worth more than money." Gram Hatter makes a heart-shaped hat for Kat.

I almost forgot. All clean-up volunteers get a coupon.

Kat looks at the paper. It's not green like a dollar bill or shiny like coins.

What's a coupon worth?

For Creative Minds

This For Creative Minds educational section contains activities to engage children in learning while making it fun at the same time. The activities build on the underlying subjects introduced in the story. While older children may be able to do these activities on their own, we encourage adults to work with the young children in their lives. Even if the adults have long forgotten or never learned this information, they can still work through the activities and be experts in their children's eyes! Exposure to these concepts at a young age helps to build a strong foundation for easier comprehension later in life. This section may be photocopied or printed from our website by the owner of this book for educational, non-commercial uses. Cross-curricular teaching activities for use at home or in the classroom, interactive quizzes, and more are available online. Go to www.ArbordalePublishing.com and click on the book's cover to explore all the links.

On the Money

Money is used to buy things. Money can come in all different shapes and sizes. In the United States of America, money is made of paper (bills) or metal (coins). The most common coins are pennies, nickels, dimes, and quarters. There are also half-dollar and dollar coins.

The coin with the smallest value is a penny. A penny is worth 1 cent (¢). It takes one hundred pennies to equal a dollar ($). A penny's value can be written as 1¢ or $0.01.

You can add up coins to make different values. A nickel and two dimes have the same value as five nickels or one quarter—25¢.

Each coin has a "head" side and a "tail" side. All coins have a president's face on the "head" side. Look below to see what each of the different coins looks like, how much it is worth, and what president is on it.

penny		$0.01 or 1¢	Abraham Lincoln 16th president, 1861—1865
nickel		$0.05 or 5¢	Thomas Jefferson 3rd president, 1801—1809
dime		$0.10 or 10¢	Franklin D. Roosevelt 32nd president, 1933—1945
quarter		$0.25 or 25¢	George Washington 1st president, 1789—1797

E Pluribus Unum. This Latin phrase is on all coins in the United States of America. It says "Out of many, one." This means that out of the many states and many different people in the USA, we all come together to make one country.

Decimal Place Value

Money can be counted in whole dollars or in parts of a dollar. There are bills worth $1, $5, $10, $20, or even $50 or $100. These bills represent whole numbers. Money can also be counted in parts of a dollar, or fractions. The **place value** after the decimal point shows parts of a number. You need these place values to represent coins, such as pennies, nickels, dimes, and quarters. Place value helps determine how big or small the value of a digit is.

Place value matters when you count whole numbers. In the number 172, the digit "1" is in the **hundreds** place. It means there is one group of one hundred. The digit "7" is in the **tens** place. It means that there are seven groups of ten—seventy. The digit "2" is in the **ones** place. It means that there are two ones—two.

Place values can also show parts of a whole number. You can imagine all whole numbers as having a decimal point followed by zeros. One dollar can be written as $1 or $1.00. The first place to the right of the decimal is the **tenths** place. The second space to the right of the decimal is the **hundredths** place.

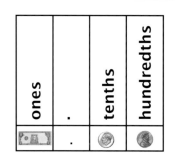

ones	.	tenths	hundredths

A penny is worth one-hundredth of a dollar. One-hundredth can be written as a fraction: $1/100$. Or it can be written as a decimal with the "1" in the hundredths place: 0.01. *If you had seven pennies, how would you write that as a fraction of a dollar? How would you write it as a decimal?*

A dime is worth one-tenth of a dollar. One-tenth can be written as a fraction: $1/10$. Or one-tenth can be written as a decimal with "1" in the tenths place: 0.1. *If you had three dimes, how would you write that as a fraction of a dollar? How would you write it as a decimal?*

Twenty-five cents goes into one dollar (or one hundred cents) exactly four times, so a quarter is worth one-fourth of a dollar. A quarter can be written as a fraction $25/100$ that is reduced to $1/4$. Or it can be written as a decimal place with "2" in the tenths place and "5" in the hundredths place: 0.25. This is the same as two dimes plus five pennies. *Why do you think a quarter is called a quarter? Hint: what is a synonym for one-fourth?*

In this chart, each number has one digit "1." Identify the place value of each digit "1."

hundreds	tens	ones	.	tenths	hundredths
1	7	2	.	0	0
0	3	6	.	1	2
0	1	5	.	0	3
3	9	6	.	1	4
1	2	3	.	0	0
0	1	2	.	3	0
0	0	1	.	2	3

Answers: 172—hundreds. 36.12—tenths. 15.03—tens. 396.14—tenths. 123—hundreds. 12.3—tens. 1.23—ones.

Counting Coins

Match the groups of coins on the left to their values on the right. Answers are below.

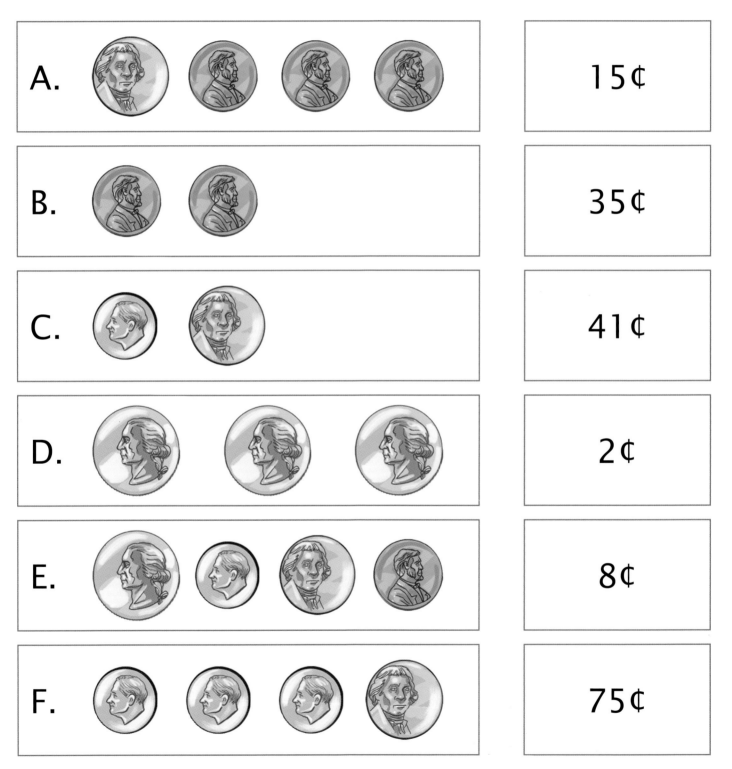

A.	15¢
B.	35¢
C.	41¢
D.	2¢
E.	8¢
F.	75¢

Answers: A = 8¢. B = 2¢. C = 15¢. D = 75¢. E = 41¢. F = 35¢.

Clean it up

Litter is any type of human-made trash that is put in a place it doesn't belong. Plants and animals—including humans—need a healthy and clean environment to live. When people litter, it hurts the environment and creates an unhealthy habitat for plants and animals.

When animals eat litter, they can choke, get sick, or die. Animals can be injured or trapped by litter. As the litter breaks down (decomposes), the pieces enter the soil. Plants can get sick or die. Animals that eat these plants can also get sick or die.

Where does trash belong?
- recycling bin
- trash can
- compost heap
- landfill
- reuse facility
- waste-to-energy plant

You can help protect the environment by not littering and by cleaning up litter wherever you see it.

Always put your trash in the proper place. Some materials—like paper, plastic, and metal—can be easily recycled and should be put in a recycle bin. Many food scraps can be composted to return nutrients to the soil. Other garbage should go into a trash can.

If you see litter, clean it up! Be careful; you don't want to cut yourself on any sharp edges. Wear gloves or use a "pick up stick" when you pick up litter. Don't put your hands in places you can't see.

type of litter	time to decompose
paper towel	2-4 weeks
cigarette	1-5 years
plastic bags	10-20 years
styrofoam cup	50 years
tire	50-80 years
plastic forks	100 years
soda can	80-200 years
plastic water bottle	450 years
disposable diaper	450 years
fishing line	600 years
glass bottles	1,000,000 years

To my grandson, Nikoli, who inspired this book when we played the "money game" and walked in nature picking up litter.—LJS

For Grandma Snyder—CW

Thanks to Rachel Hilchey, elementary math teacher with Hallsville ISD (TX), for verifying the accuracy of the information in this book.

Library of Congress Cataloging-in-Publication Data

Names: Singleton, Linda Joy, author. | Wald, Christina, illustrator.
Title: Cash Kat / by Linda Joy Singleton ; illustrated by Christina Wald.
Description: Mt. Pleasant, SC : Arbordale Publishing, [2016]. | Summary:
   While helping Gram Hatter clean up the park, Kat learns about the
   different coins she finds and hopes to uncover enough money to buy ice
   cream at the end of the day. Includes activities.
Identifiers: LCCN 2015034837 (print) | LCCN 2015041619 (ebook) | ISBN
   9781628557282 (english hardcover) | ISBN 9781628557350 (english pbk.) |
   ISBN 9781628557497 (english downloadable ebook) | ISBN 9781628557633
   (english interactive dual-language ebook) | ISBN 9781628557428 (spanish
   pbk.) | ISBN 9781628557565 (spanish downloadable ebook) | ISBN
   9781628557701 (spanish interactive dual-language ebook) | ISBN
   9781628557497 (English Download) | ISBN 9781628557633 (Eng. Interactive) |
   ISBN 9781628557565 (Spanish Download) | ISBN 9781628557701 (Span.
   Interactive)
Subjects: | CYAC: Money--Fiction. | Litter (Trash)--Fiction. |
   Parks--Fiction. | Cats--Fiction.
Classification: LCC PZ7.S6177 Cas 2016 (print) | LCC PZ7.S6177 (ebook) | DDC
   [E]--dc23
LC record available at http://lccn.loc.gov/2015034837

Translated into Spanish: *Elena Efectivo*
Lexile® Level: AD 550
key phrases: add/subtract, character, counting, currency, environment,
litter, math symbols (currency, decimals, fractions), place values

Text Copyright 2016 © by Linda Joy Singleton
Illustration Copyright 2016 © by Christina Wald

The "For Creative Minds" educational section may be copied by the owner
for personal use or by educators using copies in classroom settings.

Manufactured in China, December 2015
This product conforms to CPSIA 2008
First Printing

Arbordale Publishing
Mt. Pleasant, SC 29464
www.ArbordalePublishing.com

3 9082 13112 8152